Amy's Show-and-Tell
秀寶貝‧說故事

Coleen Reddy　著

倪靖、郜欣、王平　繪

蘇秋華　譯

三民書局

Tuesday was a big day for Amy. It was a big day for everyone, but for Amy, it was a very big day.

Tuesday was "Show-and-Tell", when all the students had to bring something to class and talk about it for three minutes. Every year, students brought the same boring stuff like doll collections or comic book collections. Some students even brought their pets. But Amy wanted to do something special this year, something that would surprise everyone. She didn't tell anyone about it. It was a big secret. If anyone knew, then the surprise would be ruined.

4

The show-and-tell began. Mr. Peemple, the teacher, said that Jason was first. Jason walked to the front of the classroom and said, "Good morning everyone. Today I would like to show you my new sneakers."

Jason took his sneakers off his feet and held them in his hands.

"They were very expensive," he continued. "They cost $140. They're very special because only a limited number of them are made. If you try to buy them now, they will be sold out. The best thing about them is the purple springs at the bottom of the shoes. When I walk or run they make a cool sound: 'Boing! Boing! Boing!'"

"Aah!" said all the students.

"Watch this," said Jason.

He put his shoes on and started jumping up and down.

"Can you hear it?" he asked eagerly.

Everybody laughed nervously because the truth was that no one could hear it. Amy rolled her eyes. She thought that Jason was really boring and vain. Who cared about his dumb sneakers?

Next, it was David's turn. David was a little
geeky but he wasn't vain like Jason.
He had a bowl of water and some fish
were swimming in the water.

"Um, um, good morning everyone. Today I would like to talk about my goldfish. I have two. Um, they're called goldfish because they're kind of gold in color. I've had many goldfish but they usually die after a few months. When they die, I flush them down the toilet.

"Their names are Seven and Eight. Because I've had so many goldfish and they all look the same, I just number them. Their numbers are their names.

I don't think goldfish are very smart because they just swim around in a bowl the whole day. I think they have boring lives. Well, that's all," he said. Then he sat down.

Amy wanted to laugh when David was doing his show-and-tell, but that would be rude. She could hear some other students laughing.

After some time, Mr. Peemple finally said, "Amy Smith."
Amy got up and went to the front of the classroom.
"Good morning," she said. "For my show-and-tell, I
brought someone that everyone has heard about but no
one has ever seen, except me. Most people are afraid of
it and would faint or scream if they saw one. So, please
don't faint or scream when you see what I've brought. Just
remember, it's very friendly and it isn't dangerous. Oh,
and you can ask it questions if you want to."
Everyone was whispering. What was Amy talking about?

Amy yelled loudly, "Mr. Dead, you can come in now."
The door opened and in walked a GHOST! It was covered
in a white sheet, and it had no feet because it wasn't
walking, but gliding across the floor. A girl started
screaming.

"Don't be stupid!" said Jason. "Of course it isn't real; it's just a prank."

"Don't be so sure," said the ghost in a deep scary voice.

"Okay everyone, you can ask him questions if you want to. His name is Mr. Dead. Don't ask him where he comes from because I promised to keep that a secret if he came to my show-and-tell," said Amy calmly.

Someone asked, "How old are you?"

"I am three hundred years old," said the ghost.

"Are you dead or alive?" asked David.

"I am not dead or alive. I am undead!" the ghost said.

"Why don't you have feet?" asked Mr. Peemple.

"I lost them one day. I took them off because they hurt and I couldn't find them after that. I don't really miss them," said Mr. Dead.

"Well, I have to finish this now because my time is up. Thank you everyone," said Amy.

Everyone started clapping and Amy was about to sit down when Mr. Peemple said, "Amy, that was lots of fun, but why don't you show us who Mr. Dead really is? I don't want anyone having nightmares tonight."

"What do you mean,
Mr. Peemple? I don't understand,"
said Amy, looking a bit scared.
"We know that Mr. Dead isn't a real ghost, so who is it?"
asked Mr. Peemple.
"He is a real ghost," insisted Amy.
"Where's this 'ghost' from? A haunted house?" asked
Mr. Peemple. Everyone started laughing but Mr. Peemple
wasn't laughing. He looked cross. His eyebrows were raised
and his face was turning red.

"I told you. I promised him I wouldn't say where he was from. You wouldn't want me to break a promise, would you?" asked Amy.

Everyone was listening to Amy and Mr. Peemple, wondering what would happen next. Mr. Dead was just standing in the corner. He wasn't moving or talking. He really did look dead.

"Okay Amy, that's enough. Pull off that white sheet!" said Mr. Peemple. He looked like a volcano that was about to explode.

What would Amy do now? Would she pull off the white sheet and reveal who Mr. Dead really was? All eyes were on Amy.

Amy looked unsure.

Suddenly, Amy turned to Mr. Dead and yelled, "Go! Get out of here before they catch you!"

Mr. Dead started moving quickly towards the door and
Mr. Peemple started running after him. But Mr. Peemple
was too late. Mr. Dead had disappeared down the
corridor.

"Sit down, Amy! I want to see you after class," said Mr. Peemple.

"Yes, Mr. Peemple," said Amy quietly. She knew she would be in trouble, but it didn't matter. Watching Mr. Peemple run after Mr. Dead was very funny and worth the trouble she would be in.

Ten minutes later, when Angela was doing her show-and-tell, there was a knock on the door.

"Come in," said Mr. Peemple.

The door opened and in walked the strangest thing. It was Mr. Stern, the principal. He wasn't alone. He was dragging someone along by the ear. It was Jack, Amy's older brother. He had a pair of roller-blades on and a white sheet in his hand.

"Look at what I found in the hallway. Instead of being in his math class, I found him roller-blading in the hallway. Everyone knows that roller-blades are not allowed in school. When I asked him what he was doing, he said that he was doing a show-and-tell for your class. Is that true, Mr. Peemple?" asked the principal.

"So you're Mr. Dead," said Mr. Peemple, looking at Jack.

"Um, yes," said Jack.

"What's going on here?" asked Mr. Stern.

Everyone thought Mr. Peemple would tell Mr. Stern everything. Amy had played a prank on the class by pretending that Jack, her brother, was a ghost and Jack helped her. Jack used roller-blades so that it would look like he had no legs. He covered himself in a white sheet so that everyone would think that he was a scary ghost. If Mr. Peemple told Mr. Stern everything, Amy and Jack would be in a lot of trouble.

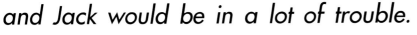

"Well, Mr. Stern, Jack is right. He was helping one of my students do a show-and-tell about roller-blades and he was just showing everyone how they worked," said Mr. Peemple. Wow, Mr. Peemple lied to the principal so that Amy and Jack wouldn't be in trouble. Mr. Peemple wasn't so bad after all.

"Okay then," said Mr. Stern. He let go of Jack's ear, which was red, and walked out of the classroom.

Jack looked embarrassed and didn't know what to say.

Just then, the bell rang and class was over. Everyone walked out until only Amy, Jack, and Mr. Peemple were left in the classroom.

"Well, Amy and Jack, what do you have to say for yourselves?" asked Mr. Peemple.

"I'm sorry. Show-and-tell is so boring; I was trying to make it a little more interesting, I guess," said Amy quietly.

"I'm sorry, too. I only did it because Amy said she would pay me $10," said Jack.

"I'll let it pass this time, but don't ever do something like this again," said Mr. Peemple.

Amy and Jack walked out of the classroom slowly. Outside all the students were waiting to see what would happen to Amy.

"Amy, I really liked your show-and-tell," said David.

"Me too, it was totally cool," said Jason.

"Thank you," said Amy. She felt a lot better.

"I wonder what I'll do next year? Something even better. Something that will knock their socks off," Amy thought to herself as she walked home.

對愛玫來說，星期二是個大日子。當然其他人也覺得這個日子很重要，但它在愛玫心目中可是個驚天動地的大日子。星期二要舉行「秀寶貝，說故事」，全部學生都得帶自己的寶貝來學校，然後用三分鐘來介紹它。年復一年，同學帶來的東西都乏善可陳，像自己收藏的洋娃娃或漫畫書什麼的，有人甚至連寵物也搬上台。今年愛玫想嘗試點不一樣的，看能不能嚇大家一跳。不論向誰她都不肯吐露半個字，這是個天大的秘密，要是被人曉得了，那可就不好玩了。

(p.1～p.3)

「秀寶貝，說故事」的時間開始了，皮波老師指定杰生先上台。杰生走到台前，開口說：「老師，各位同學，早安。我今天要秀給各位看的是我的新球鞋。」

他動手脫下球鞋，拿在手上。

然後他繼續說：「這雙鞋很貴，一雙要一百四十塊美金，它們很特別，因為是限量生產的。如果你現在想買，根本買不到了。這雙鞋最棒的地方，在於鞋底加了紫色的彈簧。所以我在走路或跑步的時候，會聽到鞋子發出『ㄅㄨㄞ・ㄅㄨㄞ・ㄅㄨㄞ』的聲音，酷吧！」

「哇！」大家齊聲讚嘆。

「注意了。」杰生說。

他穿上球鞋，開始蹦蹦跳跳。

「聽到了嗎？」他熱切地詢問大家。

同學們不自在地笑了起來，因為事實上他們什麼都沒聽到。愛玫忍不住翻了翻白眼，覺得杰生真的是無聊透頂又愛慕虛榮，誰理他那雙爛球鞋啊？

(p.5～p.7)

42

接下來輪到大維了。大維這個人有點怪，不過不像杰生那麼愛吹噓就是了。他捧著一缸水，裡面有幾條魚。

「呃……嗯……大家早。今天我想講的是我的金魚。我有兩隻金魚，呃……他們之所以叫金魚是因為身體是金色的。我養過很多金魚，不過通常活不過幾個月。如果魚死了，我就把牠們丟到沖水馬桶沖掉。」

「牠們一隻叫小七，一隻叫小八。因為我養過的金魚太多了，而且又都長得一樣，所以我乾脆用數字來幫牠們取名字，是第幾隻就叫第幾個號碼。我覺得金魚應該不是很聰明，因為牠們整天只會在魚缸裡面游來游去，我想牠們的生活大概很無趣吧。呃，我說完了。」演講完畢，大維趕緊坐下。

大維在演講的時候，愛玟很想笑，可是這樣取笑別人實在太不禮貌了。不過她還是聽到其他人在偷笑。

（p.8～p.11）

等了好一陣子，皮波老師總算點到愛玫‧史密斯。

愛玫站起來，走到講台上。

「大家早，」她說：「為了今天的『秀寶貝，說故事』，我特地帶了一個人來和大家見面，這個人也許大家都聽說過，但除了我以外，沒有人見過他。大多數的人都怕他，萬一親眼看到他，八成會尖叫或昏倒。所以，請各位看到我帶來的人時，千萬別昏倒，也不要尖叫。只要記得，他很友善，而且一點兒也不危險。喔，對了，你們如果有問題要問他的話，歡迎提出來。」

同學在底下竊竊私語。愛玫到底在說什麼啊？

愛玫大喊：「死神先生，請進！」

門一打開，走進來的居然是『鬼』！他全身覆蓋著白布，沒有腳，因為他不是用走的，而是滑進來的。一個女孩開始尖叫。

杰生說：「別傻了！那當然是假的，愛玫在惡作劇啦！」

但是鬼卻用低沈恐怖的嗓音回答他：「話可別說得太滿。」

愛玫沈著地說：「好了，各位同學，你們可以問他問題了，他叫死神先生，但是請別問他是從哪裡來的，因為我邀請他來的時候，跟他約好要保守這個秘密。」

（p.13～p.19）

一個人開口問：「你幾歲？」

「我三百歲了。」鬼回答。

大維問：「那你是死人還是活人？」

「我既不是死人也不是活人，我能超越生死。」這是鬼的回答。

皮波老師問：「你為什麼沒有腳？」

死神先生說：「搞丟了。有一天我因為腳痛，把腳拿下來，後來就找不到了，不過我倒是無所謂。」

他說完，愛玫便接著說：「好，到此為止，我的時間已經到了，謝謝各位。」

在大家的掌聲中，愛玫準備回座，但這個時候皮波老師卻問她：「愛玫，剛才真的很有趣，可是妳要不要告訴大家死神先生究竟是誰扮的呢？我不希望今天晚上有人做惡夢。」

「老師，你這句話是什麼意思？我不懂。」愛玫的表情有點害怕。

皮波老師再問一遍：「我們都知道死神先生不是真的鬼，他是誰？」

「他真的是鬼。」愛玫很堅持。

「那這個『鬼』是哪裡來的呢？鬼屋嗎？」皮波老師的話把大家逗笑了，可是皮波老師不覺得這有什麼好笑。他看起來很生氣，滿臉通紅，眉毛抬得老高。

「我說過，我跟他約好不能說他是從哪裡來的，你不會要我毀約吧，老師？」愛玫說。

（p.19～p.23）

大家都注意聽著愛玫和皮波老師的對話，等著看接下來的好戲。

死神先生只是安安靜靜，一動也不動地站在角落，看起來真的跟死了沒兩樣。

「好了，愛玫，妳鬧夠了吧，把他的白布拉下來！」皮波老師看起來好像一座即將爆發的火山。

所有的目光都盯著愛玫，看她會有什麼反應。她會把白布拉下來，揭開死神先生的真面目嗎？

愛玫顯得遲疑不定。

說時遲，那時快，愛玫轉頭向死神先生大叫：「快跑，別讓他們捉到你！」

死神先生立刻迅速向門口移動，而皮波老師也開始追著他跑。但終究慢了一步，死神先生早已消失在走廊的盡頭。

「愛玫，坐下！放學後來找我。」皮波老師說。

愛玫小聲說「好」，她知道自己有麻煩了，不過不要緊，看到皮波老師追死神的樣子真是有趣，就算惹上麻煩也值得。

（p.23～p.26）

十分鐘後，輪到安琪拉秀她的寶貝時，門口響起一陣敲門聲。

皮波老師說了聲：「請進。」

門一打開，同學們看到一幅古怪至極的景象——站在門口的是嚴校長。不過不是只有他一個人，他還揪著另一個人的耳朵，而那個人正是愛玫的哥哥傑克。他腳上穿著一雙直排輪鞋，手上還抱著一團白布。

校長問：「大家看看我在走廊上碰到誰，他沒去上數學課，卻穿著直排輪在走廊上溜冰。大家都曉得直排輪鞋是不能穿來學校的，我問他在做什麼，他說他來你們班的『秀寶貝，說故事』表演，是真的嗎？皮波老師？」

皮波老師上下打量著傑克，說：「所以你就是死神先生啊。」

「嗯……對啦。」傑克回答。

嚴校長納悶地問：「這裡發生了什麼事？」

大家都以為皮波老師會一五一十向嚴校長告狀，說愛玫對班上同學惡作劇，把傑克假扮成鬼，傑克為了幫她，特地穿上直排輪，好讓自己看起來好像沒有腳，然後用白布把自己包起來，這樣所有人都會以為他是可怕的鬼。要是皮波老師把這一切全抖出來，愛玫和傑克可慘了。

可是皮波老師卻說：「嚴校長，傑克說的並沒有錯。他是幫我們班上一個學生表演他的『秀寶貝，說故事』，我的學生要秀的寶貝是直排輪，傑克是來為大家示範直排輪要怎麼玩的。」

哇！為了愛玫和傑克，皮波先生居然向嚴校長說謊，這下子愛玫和傑克不會有事了。可見他人也不是那麼壞嘛。

(p.27～p.33)

47

嚴校長聽到皮波先生的話，說聲「那麼，好吧。」就放開傑克的耳朵，然後走出教室。大家看到傑克的耳朵紅通通的。

傑克看起來很不好意思，不曉得該說什麼才好。就在這個時候，鈴聲響起，下課了。大家都離開教室，只留下愛玫、傑克，和皮波老師在裡面。

「好了，愛玫，傑克你們有什麼話要說？」皮波老師先開口。

愛玫低聲地說：「老師，對不起，我覺得『秀寶貝，說故事』太無聊了，我只是想讓它變得有趣一點。」

傑克接著說：「我也很抱歉，我會這麼做完全是因為愛玫答應給我十塊錢。」

「這次就原諒你們，可是下回不可以再犯了。」皮波老師告誡他們。

愛玫和傑克緩緩走出教室。全班同學都在外面等他們，想知道愛玫受到什麼樣的懲罰。

大維說：「愛玫，我真的很喜歡妳的表演。」

杰生也說：「我也是，簡直酷斃了。」

愛玫說了聲：「謝謝你們。」她覺得心裡好過多了。

回家的路上，愛玫心想：「明年要做什麼才好呢？一定要來點更棒的，非把他們嚇得哇哇叫不可。」

(p.33～p.39)

波波 唸翻天系列

你知道可愛的小兔子也會 "碎碎唸" 嗎？
波波就是這樣。
他將要告訴我們什麼有趣的故事呢？

波波的復活節／波波的西部冒險記／波波上課記
我愛你，波波／波波的下雪天／波波郊遊去
波波打球記／聖誕快樂，波波／波波的萬聖夜

共 9 本，每本均附 CD

國家圖書館出版品預行編目資料

Amy's Show-and-Tell:秀寶貝，說故事 / Coleen
Reddy著；倪靖, 郜欣, 王平繪；蘇秋華譯.－－初版
一刷.－－臺北市；三民，2002
　　面；公分－－(愛閱雙語叢書. 青春記事簿系列)
中英對照
ISBN 957-14-3656-9　　(平裝)

805

© **Amy's Show-and-Tell**
　　──秀寶貝，說故事

著作人　Coleen Reddy
繪　圖　倪靖　郜欣　王平
譯　者　蘇秋華
發行人　劉振強
著作財
產權人　三民書局股份有限公司
　　　　臺北市復興北路三八六號
發行所　三民書局股份有限公司
　　　　地址／臺北市復興北路三八六號
　　　　電話／二五○○六六○○
　　　　郵撥／○○○九九九八──五號
印刷所　三民書局股份有限公司
門市部　復北店／臺北市復興北路三八六號
　　　　重南店／臺北市重慶南路一段六十一號
初版一刷　西元二○○二年十一月
編　號　S 85617
定　價　新臺幣參佰伍拾元整
行政院新聞局登記證局版臺業字第○二○○號

ISBN　957-14-3656-9　　(平裝)